Welcome to the Clown Motel

A Valentine's Day Slasher

Twyla Menezes

WELCOME TO
THE CLOWN MOTEL

A VALENTINES DAY SLASHER
TWYLA MENEZES

Copyright © 2025 by Twyla Menezes

All rights reserved.

No part of this publication may be reproduced, distributed, or transmitted in any form or by any means, including photocopying, recording, or other electronic or mechanical methods, without the prior written permission of the publisher, except as permitted by U.S. copyright law. For permission requests, contact Twyla Menezes at twylaswriting@gmail.com

The story, all names, characters, and incidents portrayed in this production are fictitious. No identification with actual persons (living or deceased), places, buildings, and products is intended or should be inferred.

Book Cover by Twyla Menezes

First edition 2025

Maple Ridge Duet:
The Scholars Gambit
Book 2 -TBA

Anthology:
Hallow 13

Short Stories:
The Lurkers: A Short Story of Maggie & Harold

"Guess that's why we all hold onto life so hard....Even the dead....We're all just scared of the unknown."
— Sam Winchester, Supernatural, Season 2: Roadkill

Content Advisory

Welcome to the Clown Motel! I'm thrilled you decided to stay the night, but before you enter here's a little content advisory for you.

Gore – Death – Violence – Possession — and yes Clowns.

Part One

Friends In The Dark

The Clown Motel's parking lot stretched before them, a vast and desolate expanse under the mid-afternoon sun. An unsettling silence hung in the air, broken only by the faint rustle of leaves that seemed to whisper warnings. Reena shot a concerned glance at Nasha, her worry deepening as she caught sight of Nasha's ashen face. They had been inseparable since high school, best friends turned lovers during their junior year, but this venture beyond the realm threatened to fracture the foundation they had built together.

While Reena thrived on the thrill of the paranormal, Nasha's eyes betrayed a growing unease. She had always been terrified of clowns, a phobia that wasn't easily shaken, and now they were sitting before an old motel notorious for its ghostly tales and sinister history. The discussion to come here had nearly spiraled into a fierce argument; Reena had almost lost her nerve, unsure if Nasha would be there to support her when it mattered most.

Nasha remained silent, her gaze fixated on the ominous structure that loomed ahead. Reena bit her lip, her pulse quickening as she took in the grotesque sight of the motel. The building was a garish deep red, its paint peeling and faded as if it, too, were a relic of nefarious memories long past. A gaudy display of colorful dots freckled the exterior, but they did little to mask the sinister atmosphere that seeped from its walls. A towering clown sign loomed about the rooftop, its eyes peering into your soul, and its painted grin was now cracked and dulled by harsh seasons. The sign creaked in the relentless breeze, sounding more like a warning than a welcome, casting eerie shadows stretching like grasping hands into the gathering dusk.

Goosebumps rose on Reena's arms as she contemplated the secrets within the grim facade. The weight of the place seemed to press down on her, suffocating her excitement with a sense of dread. She swallowed hard against the lump in her throat, her heart pounding as she unbuckled her seatbelt, steeling herself for whatever nightmares awaited them inside.

"Babe, are we really going to do this?" Nasha chewed her long, black-painted nails, glancing nervously toward the endless stretch of barren land outside the car window.

Reena nodded as she reached into the backseat for her

dark green equipment bag, its straps worn and faded from years of use. The air felt thick and oppressive as if the whole world held its breath. The only signs of life were a clump of tumbleweeds and the distant whisper of the wind, which seemed to carry faint, ghostly echoes.

"Fine." Nasha scoffed, her voice quivering slightly as she undid her belt and grabbed the other bag. "But if shit gets weird, we're going home—no questions."

"Deal." Reena tucked a lock of her purple-tipped blonde hair behind her ear, her heart pounding in rhythm with the eerie silence. She let out a slow, steady breath and pushed open the car door.

Warm, sticky heat clung to her skin, and Nasha's face scrunched as she slammed the door shut behind them, echoing ominously in the stagnant air. She stood, fixated on the peeling, yellow entrance door, which seemed to grimace back at her. Reena noticed neither dared to step toward the unsettling building, an unnatural chill creeping up their spines despite the humidity.

Nasha stole a glance at Reena, her expression hardening. "Let's get this done. I don't like the vibe here."

Trying to lighten the mood, Reena mouthed the words 'I love you' before swinging her backpack around. With a deliberate motion, she revealed a clunky old camera, its lens glinting like a watchful eye. As she powered it on, a light whirring filled the air.

The bag swung back around, landing softly on her back.

She forced a smile into the camera, the brightness of her excitement clashing with the creeping shadows. "Welcome to Friends in the Dark." Reena approached Nasha, taking each step measuredly and almost hesitantly. "I'm Reena."

"And I'm Nasha," she said, waving.

"Tonight, we will be staying in the Clown Motel," Reena declared, flipping the camera to show the grotesque facade of the building before them. Its chipped paint and clown eyes were watching. "So let's get started."

"Wait." Reena squealed. "You guys! We can see the cemetery from here." She pointed toward the plot of land encircled by a white picket fence, the mid-afternoon sun casting long shadows that seemed to reach for them. "This is going to be a good night."

Nasha folded her arms tighter across her chest, her bravado wavering. "Dear beloved followers," she blurted, the words slipping out uneasily. Reena panned the camera back to Nasha, capturing her hesitant smile. "Reena is crazy for this. So you better give this a thumbs up and subscribe if you haven't already—if you dare."

"Haha. It's going to be fun," Reena said, though the tremor in her voice betrayed her. She took a tentative step toward the door as if crossing a threshold that would change them forever. "Are you ready?"

Nasha shook her head no but placed a foot before her. Slowly, they put one foot in front of the other and opened the intimidating yellow door. Reena pointed the camera at the floor so the manager wouldn't know she was recording, just in case he wasn't okay with it. As she slowly approached the counter, a man with tan skin and short black hair sat on a stool leaning against it, smiling.

"Welcome to the Clown Motel. I'm Bobby, the owner." He smiled, placing his chin on his hands.

Reena watched Nasha explore the room, her eyes darting from one colorful, glass-clown figurine to another. Each piece shimmered under the soft glow of the overhead lights, reflecting a kaleidoscope of colors that danced across the walls. In the center of the room stood a giant doll, its painted smile and extravagant costume drawing Nasha's attention like a magnet.

Reena's heart raced as she took in the scene—shelves lined from floor to ceiling, crammed with an eclectic collection of whimsical glass creations, each unique and meticulously crafted. When she finally realized that not even a tiny space remained for a single additional figurine, her eyes widened in astonishment. It was as if the room had been swallowed by the very essence of clowns and dolls, leaving no room for anything new, only a vivid tapestry of memories and stories waiting to be discovered.

Bobby chuckled. "Is this your first time staying here?"

Nasha nodded, glancing around the dimly lit room, shadows stretching unnaturally along the walls. "Yeah. Can you give us some history of the place?"

Reena hesitated, holding up her camera, a faint tremor

in her hand. "And can I record you for our channel?"

"Sure, sure," he said, his smile fading slightly. "I'm guessing you are paranormal investigators?" He gestured for them to follow, his movements almost too eager.

"We are." Reena beamed. "How long have you been collecting clowns for?"

"That sounds fun," Bobby replied, his smile widening but not reaching his eyes. He walked to a dusty case filled with clown figurines, pausing as he pointed out a few. "I've been collecting clown dolls, figurines, and paintings since I was fourteen."

"Fourteen? That's pretty young."

"Yes, I went to a circus with my family ... the laughter and colors were intoxicating. But this place—well, it found me in 2019. I bought it after the last owner ... disappeared. We're not quite sure what happened."

He gestured toward his favorite pieces, their cracked porcelain faces adorned with droopy, sorrowful expressions. But his eyes gleamed with a strange fervor as he focused on one particular doll—a towering figure standing six feet tall in the middle of the main office. "This is Willie the Clown," he said, his voice whispering as he pointed to the lifelike doll, its glassy eyes seeming to watch them intently.

In the silence that followed, they could almost hear the faint echo of distant laughter chilling in the still air. Nasha reached up to stroke the doll's cheek and visibly shivered. The doll wore a red pointy hat, a half-red suit with half-colored strips, and huge, shiny red shoes. Willie looked too human-like for Reena's comfort. It left a feeling Reena couldn't understand, swirling in the pit of her stomach.

Reena narrowed her eyes at Nasha, whose eyes seemed so keen on something she was terrified of, showing her future viewers this bizarre clown. "Wow, his hands are huge. Everyone, say hi to Willie, the clown." She pointed the camera down at his vast feet and slowly moved it up his body toward his tall, pointed hat. His eyes were painted so well she swore they were peering into her soul.

"And when did you get him?" Reena asked.

"Yeah, he was already here when I bought the place," the owner replied, his smile stretching slightly too wide.

"Already here?" Reena panned the camera back to Bobby.

"When I bought the place, there were eight hundred clown figurines—eight hundred clowns. Can you imagine?" He chuckled. "I had two hundred figurines, but people have brought theirs too. It's grown to over two thousand clowns in my collection," he said, his eyes gleaming.

"That's wild," Nasha whispered, her voice trembling slightly as she glanced nervously at the clown. Then, she dropped her eyes to the life-like hand of the figurine before she reached out and grabbed it.

"Stop touching it," Reena whispered urgently, her heart

racing.

"It's just a doll," Nasha scoffed as an unsettling shiver passed through her.

"Says the skeptic," Reena shot back, her eyes wide as they circled back to the counter, where the weight of unblinking clown eyes seemed to press down on them like an unshakable shadow.

Nasha shrugged.

"How do you feel about your passion becoming a place where people explore the paranormal?" Reena bit her lip, hoping she wasn't pushing too hard.

Bobby sat back on his stool with a sigh. "At first, I was upset by this," he murmured, his voice barely above a whisper as he folded his arms tightly. "But then it began to bring in more people, all drawn like moths to a flame. I'm booked almost daily, sharing my love for clowns—but it feels different now." His eyes darkened, only momentarily, before he cleared his throat and smiled. "What's the name for the check-in?" Bobby moved his mouse around, illuminating the screen.

"Reena Thompson."

His eyes scanned the screen before he turned and grabbed a set of keys hanging off a wooden board behind him.

"Here are your room keys. I'll be here all night if you ladies need anything." Bobby smiled slightly.

"Thank you." Nasha grabbed the keys and opened the

door.

Reena set through, and relief flooded her chest. It was as if someone was sitting on her while she was in there. "Man. That main lobby is something else."

"This place is something else," Nasha said as she walked ahead.

Nasha and Reena strolled to the last room, 107. The room was listed on the website as Fear Unlimited. According to their research, Reena had found that room 107 was closed for the previous four years after three deaths occurred in the room over the last ten years. One death was of an older gentleman who had a heart attack, which was sad. The other two were of a lover killing their spouse—brutally. The images Reena found gave her chills.

Tyler Morse, who was alive and still in prison for killing his spouse and the other man, was a bit more brutal. A man named Amon Bellinor had stabbed his girlfriend Sarah of ten years fifteen times, and the other was of a girl who was chopped into bits and hung up like art throughout the room. Reena mentally took note of the guy's name, Amon, who had passed and was buried near the motel, but it didn't specify where precisely. Though Reena didn't get a chance to find where Amon was buried during her research, she left a sticky tab on her computer to look more into him, as his grave could be an incredible site to visit for the channel.

Guests in room 108 spoke of strange happenings—furniture dragging across the floor in the dead of night, incessant thudding against the walls, and the chilling cadence of muffled voices. Shadows flickered at the corners of their eyes. Most guests had checked out and left before the morning sun.

Meanwhile, room 107 was locked away from the world after Amon's crime, and its door was barred from guests until May 4th of this year. Those who dared to stay whispered of lingering darkness, wondering what secrets the walls of room 107 held and what fate awaited those who crossed its threshold.

Reena appeared next to Nasha and turned the camera toward them. "We are officially going to our room!"

Nasha eyed Reena as she grabbed the long metal handle, stuck the key in, and pushed open the door. "Oh hell nah!"

Reena turned slowly, her heart hammering as she showed the camera the creepy room where she was meant to stay the night. The walls were covered in brick wallpaper adorned with neon-colored clowns, their painted smiles stretching wide in manic grins. Shadows danced in the dim light, making the figures appear almost alive.

"We do this for you guys," Reena said as she continued to scan the room.

Two queen-sized beds were present, each draped in sheets with fake blood stains and matching pillows sitting at the head of each bed. A long chestnut dresser stood against the wall, its surface scarred and scratched. An old, clunky, and worn-out TV sat on top. Reena's excitement grew as the camera captured every detail of the room.

"This is creepy," Reena said, dragging out the last word, her voice barely a whisper.

Nasha shook her head, glancing uneasily around the dimly lit room. "Reena, are we doing this?"

Reena walked inside with a slight smile that felt forced, setting the recording camera on the dresser. "Time to set up, babe."

"Our Valentine's Day tomorrow better be amazing," Nasha warned, her eyes narrowing.

Reena's brow rose. "It will be. I have the whole day planned out." She placed another camera on a shelf near the bathroom door and hit record. The soft beeping echoed in the silence.

"And when will I be finding out these plans?" Nasha asked as she pulled her phone from her back pocket.

"When we get there tomorrow," Reena said as she set another camera and the large, red REM pod by the door, turning them both on, the lights flickering eerily as they came to life. "It's a surprise. I've been planning this for months."

"Good." Nasha sighed. "You're going to have a lot of making up to do."

"I know. You keep saying that." Reena turned the fourth-night vision camera slightly to the left. "Okay, the last camera is up."

"I have the reviews popped up." Nasha shook her phone.

Reena joined Nasha on the bed, kissing her cheek. "We have four cameras in every corner, and a REM pod set up. To our loyal viewers, you already know what a REM pod is, but if you are new, a REM pod detects temperature changes. I have it set up near the door. If anything gets close to it, it'll go off," Reena explained. Standing up, she demonstrated by waving her foot in front of it. The closer her leg got, the louder it went off.

Reena settled back onto the bed beside Nasha, who sat there with an expressionless gaze fixed on a spot on the wall. Concern furrowed Reena's brow as she studied Nasha, noticing the distant look in her eyes. Taking a deep breath, she reached out and gently nudged Nasha's shoulder. "Hey, are you okay?" she whispered.

Nasha cleared her throat. "Ready for the reviews?" She looked down and scrolled through her phone.

"I don't know. Maybe I'm ready for a little something else." Reena crawled toward Nasha on the bed. Nasha giggled. Reena gently kissed Nasha's pink lips as she lay backward on the bed. Reena crawled on top of her, her cool mahogany skin glowing in this dim lighting. Nasha sucked Reena's lip into her mouth before biting it playfully.

"Save this energy for tomorrow," Nasha said, laughing.

"We're going to have to cut this."

"Yeah, we are." Reena leaned toward her, leaving a trail of kisses down her neck.

Nasha suddenly sat up, her eyes darting around the dimly lit room. Shadows danced along the walls, adding to the unsettling atmosphere.

"Are you feeling okay?" Reena whispered.

"Yeah, let's just get this over with." Nasha's tone was flat, almost hollow.

"Fine," Reena replied, her heart racing as she moved to sit beside her girlfriend.

Nasha shrugged, her shoulders tense, and cleared her throat. "This motel was built over some of the cemeteries that are also part of this land."

"That's probably why it's haunted, or people claim it is."

"Okay. First review: My significant other and I stayed in room 108, and throughout the night, we heard whispering voices that seemed to creep from the walls, accompanied by faint knocks that echoed in the silence. We were jolted awake by a blood-curdling scream around 3 a.m., a sound that sliced through the night like a knife. When we rushed to the owner, he seemed unaffected, claiming he had heard nothing, as if we were lying. We couldn't stay another minute; we packed our things and fled. *November 25, 2021.*"

Nasha read on, her voice trembling as she shared more reviews that sent chills racing down Reena's spine. Tales of full-body apparitions lurking in the shadows, unexplained scratches marking the skin, and terrifying glimpses of clowns—some even wrote about Willie the Clown, claiming they saw him shift ever so slightly when they entered the main office, a sinister grin freezing on his painted face. The air around them grew colder as if the walls were listening.

Nails scraped slowly against the wall from the room over—room 108. Nasha jolted off the bed, her phone slipping from her grasp and hitting the floor with a hollow thud. "No one was in the parking lot earlier, Reena. It's just us," she whispered, her voice trembling.

Reena hopped off the bed and peeked through the grimy motel blinds. Only her battered tan car was parked in the desolate lot, but as she turned her gaze toward room 108, a series of relentless bangs reverberated through the walls, making the framed pictures quiver as if they, too, were alive.

Reena gasped, the sound escaping her lips like steam from a kettle. "We're finally getting the proof we needed," she breathed, a wild spark igniting in her eyes.

Nasha snatched her phone from the floor, heart racing, a prickling sensation creeping along her spine. "We need to go," she insisted, her voice barely above a whisper.

"What, no!?" Reena's voice was urgent as she grabbed the clunky handheld camera from the dresser, her fingers trembling with adrenaline. "This is it! We're finally capturing evidence of what's been haunting this place."

Suddenly, the banging ceased, an unnatural silence settling like a heavy shroud around them.

Nasha grabbed Reena's arm. "Reena," she whispered, a sense of foreboding rising. She dashed out of the room.

Reena turned the camera towards her, her eyes beaming. "Please tell me you guys heard that!" She giggled nervously. "I hope all that noise was caught on camera."

"You are absolutely crazy." Nasha rolled her hazel eyes as she stood by the car. "Let's go walk or something."

Reena ambled out of the room, the camera panning reluctantly towards the cemetery, its gravestones looming like silent sentinels. "With the dead?"

"I don't care at this point. I don't want to go back in that room." Nasha's voice trembled slightly, her gaze darting nervously toward the open door.

Reena smirked as she crept over to room 108, pressing the camera to the window, its glass cool against her skin. "It looks pretty empty to me. Do you guys see anything?"

"Is there really nothing in there?" Nasha leaned closer, her heart racing.

Reena shrugged, though her pulse quickened in her chest. "Nothing that I can see. Not even the camera is picking anything up."

"Did you bring the board?" Nasha's voice was barely above a whisper.

"You just said you didn't want to go back in there."

Reena's brows pinched together.

Nasha glanced toward the graveyard, the moonlight casting eerie silhouettes. "It's not midnight yet."

"So, Ouija board?" Reena flipped the camera around, her expression half-joking, yet the glint in her eyes hinted at the thrill of danger. "Friends in the Dark! Do you hear that? Nasha Stone wants to do an Ouija session."

"Shut up." Nasha rolled her eyes, though a flicker of fear washed over her. She pushed open the door to their room, peering inside into the oppressive darkness. "It's quiet now."

"Maybe the spirits don't like us digging into the past," Reena said as they crossed the threshold, the air thick with anticipation.

Nasha slowly stepped inside. "Then maybe we should wait on the board session. See if we can get them to communicate through other devices first."

Reena followed a chill creeping up her spine as she returned the camera to its resting place on the dresser, the room feeling more alive. "Yeah, let's do it."

Nasha zipped open her bag, her hands trembling slightly as she pulled out a spirit box, its surface cold and familiar. "Are we sure?"

"For the channel," Reena replied, her heart pounding, sensing something shifting in the air.

Nasha forced a quick smile, wiping her clammy hands on her pants. "For the channel."

But something felt off to Reena like a presence lingered just beyond the edges of her perception. She sat on the bed, its fabric worn and ancient, as Nasha turned on the spirit box. It crackled ominously, the sound unsettling in the thick silence. Nasha placed it carefully between them on the bed before joining Reena.

"Hello, my name is Reena, and I'm not here to hurt you."

The spirit box flickered through channels, each one more disheartening than the last, as the only reply was an unsettling static that filled the air with an eerie tension.

"And I'm Nasha. We only want to communicate."

Reena pointed to the spirit box, her heart racing. "If you wish to speak with us, use your energy to speak into this device."

Static pierced the silence.

Reena's eyes scanned the dimly lit room. Waiting. Hoping.

Silence stretched taut.

"We heard banging earlier. Was that you?"

The channels flicked, and the static soon silenced. *'No.'*

"If it wasn't you, then who was it?" Reena's brows knitted tightly.

Nasha shook her head slowly, a faint tremor in her voice. "I don't—"

'Clown.'

Nasha jumped off the bed, her face paled as the words

echoed in the stillness. "Reena. Did that just say ... clown?"

'Clown,' the spirit box scratched out again, its voice laden with menace.

Then, a devilish laugh sliced through the silence from the next room, a sound that twisted the heart and sent ice crawling up their spines. Fingers began to tap against the wall, a rhythmic crescendo that grew louder, punctuating the oppressive stillness.

Nasha turned off the spirit box, desperation lacing her voice. "What is happening?"

"I don't know," Reena whispered, her breath hitching.

The tapping abruptly stopped. The silence grew as they stared at the wall. Standing hand in hand, neither of them moved. Reena's heart beat rapidly out of her chest, ringing in her ears.

After moments of tense silence, Reena took a slow, deliberate breath and stepped toward the camera. The instant Reena's fingers grazed the camera, a deep, resounding bang echoed through the room, causing the walls to shudder. Paintings trembled, their frames buckling before crashing to the ground with a haunting thud.

Nasha's scream pierced Reena's ears as her grip tightened around Reena's arm, urgently tugging her toward the door.

Yet, amidst the chaos, Reena's determination won. She snatched the camera, allowing Nasha to pull her outside.

The moment they crossed the threshold, an eerie silence engulfed them.

"They don't want us in there, Reena," Nasha said, eyes wide with terror. "We can't go back in."

"I need to get our stuff," Reena insisted, her hands trembling, shaking the camera.

"No. We should just walk to the cemetery," Nasha said, shaking.

"The cemetery?" Reena panned the camera toward the cemetery, flicking on the light with a nervous chuckle. "Well, at least we can see."

"Yeah. Get some fresh air while I decide if I want to leave," Nasha replied, her voice faint, as if she was trying to convince herself as much as Reena. "You're lucky I love you."

"Did you hear that, everyone? She loves me." Reena's laughter broke the tension. "Let's go for a walk, and let me know what you decide."

"Maybe we should just leave now," Nasha urged, her eyes flickered between the cemetery and the car.

"Your bonnet is in there." Reena made a yikes face.

Nasha gasped. "You brought my bonnet?"

"Yeah, you always forget it, and I didn't want you to freak out about it," Reena replied, shrugging.

Nasha slowly looped her arm through Reena's, her grip filled with uncertainty. "Thank you," she murmured, casting one last look at the darkened doorway as if expecting something to emerge from the shadows.

The pavement disappeared and was replaced by rocks crunching under Reena's shoes, now sprinkled with dirt. The camera light only illuminated a limited area, leaving the rest to her imagination. The wind whipped around them furiously—no trees or buildings around to block them from the rough gusts.

A waist-height wooden fence enclosed two unmarked graves. "Who do you think is buried here?"

Nasha squatted to get a closer look. "It doesn't say anything. Just has those wooden crosses."

"Creepy." Reena drew out the ending of the word. "Maybe they were bad men."

"Maybe. It makes sense to keep them unmarked. Don't want anyone remembering who they were."

Reena sighed as she looked at the tombstones. "I wish I could have grabbed the spirit box."

Nasha reached into her pocket with a smirk. "I have it."

"You didn't put it down?" Reena chuckled.

"Hell nah. I was going to use it to bash someone's head in."

Reena laughed. "I'm going to have to cut that from the video."

Nasha shrugged. "Only speaking the truth." She flipped the switch and set it inside the wooden fence with the unmarked graves. The spirit box rapidly flipped through the radio waves.

"Are you sure?"

Nasha nodded, her black kinky curls bouncing off her shoulders. "Have to give them something other than us running out like a bunch of scared girls."

"Ha, this is true." Reena placed the camera on the tombstone next to her. "I think this should be good."

The static stopped. *'Clown.'*

"Why do you keep saying, clown?" Nasha scoffed and threw up her hands.

'Coming.'

"A clown is coming?" Reena looked around. "Is he a ghost?"

"There's no way this device keeps spitting out the word clown. It's broken."

"It said *'coming.'*"

Nasha's breath quickened as she glanced around the graveyard. "I don't see anything."

'Run.'

Nasha yelped, clutching Reena's arm tightly. "Babe."

Reena's eyes scanned the graveyard as she wrenched herself free from Nasha's clutch and hurried to grab her camera from the crumbling tombstone. She panned it around the desolate grounds. Old, moss-covered markers lay like forgotten spirits beneath tangled weeds. Their inscriptions faded over time. Just then, her camera lens caught something—a flash of red, a silky outfit peeking out from behind an ancient tree.

"Nasha," she breathed, her voice trembling as she nudged Nasha's arm. "There's someone over there."

"Where?" Nasha squinted, scanning the shadows, her heart pounding.

A head popped from behind the tree, eyes glimmering like cold stars, and the girls screamed.

"Hell no!" Nasha's grip tightened around the spirit box. "You better stay back!"

The clown's head cocked to the side. Reena could see the person was smiling from behind the mask. He took a step from behind the tree and stood there. Staring. His hands were clenching and unclenching at his sides. *The clown stood tall and slim, or maybe he was fit underneath all that and hot.* Reena pondered. *Or he was a sick older man who was going to take us to his basement and hack our bodies into tiny pieces.*

Nasha glanced over at Reena and whispered, "Run."

Reena quickly followed behind her. Nasha kicked up dirt as she took off toward the motel. Their footsteps pounded against the hardened dirt. As Reena looked back, she saw the clown taking chase, but he wasn't nearly running as fast as they were. Maybe they'd be able to take him.

"He's following us!" Renna yelled.

Nasha didn't look back at her as she pumped her arms and legs, almost leaving Reena behind. "Run, Reena!"

"I am!" she said breathlessly. One thing Reena didn't like was working out and being sweaty. It was a no-go for her. Even in high school, she failed physical education for refusing to participate in the mile run, but when her life depended on it, she could put a pep in her step.

Room 107's door came into view, and relief flooded Reena. Her lungs were on fire, and her legs wanted to collapse. Nasha shoved her golden key into the lock and pushed the door open, and fear replaced her calm eyes. "He's right behind you! Reena, run!"

Reena almost dropped the camera as she ran past her old beat-up car and into the room, collapsing on the ground and gasping for air.

Nasha slammed the door shut, quickly locking it. The door vibrated as the person on the other side banged on it. The window rattled along the wall, and then it all stopped.

"Shit, shit, shit!" Reena clutched her chest. "How are we supposed to leave? It's the middle of the night."

"We're stuck in the middle of nowhere with a clown. A damn clown."

"Hello?" The clown tapped the window. "You wanna play?"

"Go away!" Nasha's fist clenched at her sides. "I'll call the cops."

"One two ... Silly Willie wants to play with you." He laughed. "Three-four ... Can you open your door?" He cocked his head. His dark, beady eyes peered at them through the blinds.

"Did you hear us? We are calling the cops." Reena

dropped the camera onto the bed and patted her pockets for her phone, but it was gone. Her heart thundered in her chest, and her nerves crashed through her body. "I—"

"Five six …" The clown didn't finish as the bottom panel of the window was smashed in. "I just wanna play." He stuck his hand through, and a menacing laughter followed.

"Babe." Reena's eyes widened.

"What?"

"I must have dropped my phone." She began to pat her pockets once more.

"There's no way out of here." Nasha's lip quivered as she pulled her phone from her pocket. "No service."

Reena glanced at the bathroom. "Let me check for a window." She ran back to the bathroom. It only had a small vent window. Tears stung the back of her eyes. *What are we going to do? This has to be a joke.*

She stepped back into the room, shaking her head. "We wouldn't fit."

"Then we are fighting." Nasha tossed her a bedside lamp.

"Fighting?" Reena's eyes widened. "He's over six feet tall."

Something hit the ground with a loud thud.

"What the hell?" Nasha peered around and ran into the bathroom.

"What is it?"

"It's a wasp nest!" She shrieked, her hands flailing in the

air.

"What!?" Reena grabbed her stuff from around the room and her bag off the bed before running into the bathroom. "We need to leave."

"Where are we going to go?"

"There's two of us and one of him."

Nasha sighed. "Okay." She pushed open the bathroom door. "I don't hear anything."

Light buzzing filled the room.

"Oh shit! There's wasps." She slammed the door shut.

"What about your phone?" Reena's brows pinched.

Nasha reached into her back pocket. The red battery lit the screen three times before falling to a blank screen. "Fuck."

"We need to make a run for it." Reena threw her a towel. "Wrap yourself in this." Reena took a towel for herself, wrapping it around her face but leaving a small opening for her eyes. Nasha did the same.

"One, two, three." Nasha swung open the bathroom door, and they ran through the motel room together and out the door into the parking lot.

Reena clutched her bag, glancing around the empty parking lot. A slight breeze swept through, causing tumbleweeds to stroll past, but no clown was in sight. She reached into her pocket, pulled her car keys out, and opened the door. They slid into the car and locked the doors. Reena threw the bag into the backseat.

"Nasha. You didn't grab your bag."

She shook her head. "I'm not going back in."

"That's over a thousand dollars of equipment." Reena went to open her door when her car was hit with something heavy, rocking the vehicle. Reena screamed.

Nasha whipped her head around to see the clown pointing and laughing at them from behind the car. His hands clutched his stomach as he hunched over, fake laughing. His smile grew wide as he cocked his side to the side, his eyes piercing into Reena's.

"Is your door locked?" Nasha clutched onto the armrest.

Reena glanced down and hit the lock button just as the clown made his way to the front of the car. He again pointed and laughed. "Can't we play?"

"We need to leave."

Nasha shook her head. "Babe, I love you, but fuck the equipment. We can buy more. We need to leave!"

The clown turned and walked into the room. Reena started the car and slowly began to back away, the wheels crunching along the pavement. She didn't want to leave all her equipment, but she didn't want to die either. It had taken her all of high school to save money for this stuff.

He jogged up to the car, holding the broken wasp nest, and smashed it into the front window. The thud rattled the windshield, causing Reena to snap her head forward.

"I can't see!" Reena slammed on the brakes.

"Silly Willy just wants to play."

Tears swelled in Reena's eyes. "Leave us alone!"

"Play." His voice went from friendly to plain evil.

"No! We aren't going to play." Nasha's hand reached for Reena's.

Reena's fingers interlaced with hers and squeezed.

She hit the windshield wipers with her free hand, hoping they would remove the gunk stuck to them.

When she was able to peer through the windshield, another clown in a blue suit was walking their way—pointing and laughing.

Her stomach churned sour. Reena brought Nasha's hand to her dry lips and kissed it. "I'm sorry. I shouldn't have asked you to come here."

Nasha didn't reply. Reena glanced over to see her zoned out with a blank stare.

"Nasha?"

"It's okay, baby. Just slowly back up."

"Just drive backward?"

Nasha nodded. "Slowly back up."

"Okay." Renna reversed the car and slowly backed out of the empty lot.

As her car crept closer to the sidewalk, a third clown in a blue and red suit appeared, holding a baseball bat with nails sticking out of it at unusual angles.

She hit her brakes, jolting them forward.

"Why did you stop?" Nasha snapped.

"There's another clown."

Nasha peered behind her seat. "Run the motherfucker over."

"Nasha!"

"Listen, if you don't run him over and get me out of here. We are done." Nasha's voice dripped with fear, but the hint of anger hit Reena in the face.

Reena's heart sank. Nasha had never threatened their relationship before. She glanced over at Nasha, who had a bead of sweat lining her furrowed brows. She took a steady breath and slowly let her foot off the brake. The car started to roll backward, but she slammed on the brakes again.

"I'm sorry. I can't." Reena shook her head. "I can't kill someone."

"He won't die, Reena!" Nasha glanced over the headrest. "He'll be in pain, but he won't die."

She shook her head and gripped the steering wheel. "I—I can't."

The clowns closed in around them, taunting them and banging their fists on the car. Reena narrowed her eyes at the clown approaching her door. His arm stretched outward, showing off a glimpse of a tattoo.

Her brows pinched together as she intently studied the tattoo peeking out from beneath the colorful fabric of the clown's suit. A slight chuckle escaped her lips as realization dawned on her. "It's my brother?"

Nasha's head whipped around, her eyes wide. "How do

you know?" she pressed.

"Look closely at the bottom of the sleeve," Reena pointed out. "There's part of his lion tattoo peeking out."

Nasha squinted her eyes and gasped in disbelief. "Are you kidding me? That's actually him?"

Before Reena could respond, the passenger door flew open so abruptly that she barely had enough time to shift her car into park.

"Are you kidding me?!" Nasha exclaimed as she shoved the nearest clown, her frustration evident.

The clown erupted into laughter, casually peeling off his mask to reveal tousled blonde hair framing his naturally tanned skin. His vibrant green eyes sparkled with mischief and amusement.

"I almost shit my pants," Reena said through a laugh, finally joining Nasha outside the car. Her heart was still racing from the scare.

Chad doubled over laughing. Their combined laughter echoed throughout the empty parking lot. "You should have seen your faces! Priceless!"

Nasha punched him in the arm, her irritation etched into her face. "Jackass," she muttered.

Bryce sauntered over, wrapping his arm around Reena's shoulders with a casual confidence. "Nothing like a harmless prank to spice things up." He grinned.

"Yeah, well, try explaining that to Mom if I had a heart attack," Reena countered, her tone mocking as she rolled her eyes at him.

Bryce shook his head. "Always with the dramatics. Can't you take a joke?"

Reena nudged his arm away as her expression turned serious. "You chased us and threw a wasp nest in the room, remember? And you guys broke the damn window!"

"That's okay," an unfamiliar voice chimed in unexpectedly. "He'll pay for it."

"Exactly. I'll pay for it," Chad affirmed, waving off Reena's concern with a dismissive gesture. "But really, I am sorry."

"With what, daddy's money?" Nasha shot back, her sarcasm laced with indignation.

The third clown took off his mask, revealing none other than Bobby, the owner of the circus.

"What, you were in on it too?" Reena chuckled, a mix of disbelief and amusement washing over her.

"Oh yeah," Bobby laughed. "Your brother called and asked if they could play a prank, and I simply couldn't resist jumping in on the fun."

"Are you kidding?" Nasha punched Chad again.

Chad shrugged nonchalantly as he rubbed his arm. "At least I made your channel more interesting." He grinned slyly.

"You watch the channel?" Nasha narrowed her eyes.

"Yeah, and it sucks," he replied with a cheeky smirk, clearly enjoying the banter.

"I'm heading in," Bobby announced, waving cheerfully. "Thanks for letting me in on your prank. It was a good laugh."

"No problem at all," Bryce replied, returning the gesture. "Thanks again."

Chad and Bryce clasped hands, their camaraderie evident. "Man, that was a brilliant idea." Chad chuckled.

"I almost started crying," Reena admitted, folding her arms across her chest in mock annoyance.

Bryce laughed heartily. "Had to give your viewers something extra, so we did."

"I swear, if they love this collab, I'm quitting," Nasha declared, her nostrils flaring in frustration.

Brimming with energy, Reena grabbed her camera from the back seat and switched it on. "Well, Friends in the Dark, it looks like we got fooled. Until next time!" A chorus of cheerful waves greeted the camera.

"You guys suck," Reena teased, mischievously sticking her tongue out while playfully shoving Chad.

The atmosphere shifted as Reena powered off the camera, and Nasha's smile faded into a more serious expression.

"What's wrong, babe?" Reena asked, sensing Nasha's change in mood.

"That was bullshit. It wasn't funny," Nasha muttered, shaking her head as the frustration bubbled up.

Reena smiled reassuringly. "No one got hurt. Just a

prank."

But Nasha shook her head defiantly and stormed down the dimly lit street, the tension lingering in the air.

"Where are you going?" Chad chuckled.

"Nasha!" Reena called after her, throwing her hands up. "Where are you going?!"

Nasha strode away, her hips swaying as she went down the street without looking back.

"I guess we'll wait for her to come back?" Bryce suggested, rubbing the back of his neck.

Reena sighed deeply, her expression shifting to concern. "I guess so. Let me pull my car up." She slid back into the front seat of her old, beat-up car and maneuvered it into the parking spot for room 107. Exiting the vehicle, she grabbed her backpack, relieved she wouldn't have to leave her belongings behind.

"I can't believe you broke the window," Bryce said incredulously, picking up shards of glass scattered across the ground.

"I wasn't planning on it." Chad chuckled.

"You always take things too far," Reena added, her tone teasing but with a hint of sincerity.

Chad shrugged nonchalantly, a mischievous grin creeping onto his face. "Teach me how to use your equipment."

"Why?" Reena's brows pulled together.

"So I can make a channel and outshine you," he declared.

Reena playfully shoved him, her laughter ringing out. "Fuck off."

Just then, as she opened the door to room 107, a few startled wasps buzzed out, causing her to gasp.

"Here, let me clean it," Bob's voice startled her as he approached, a smile on his face.

"Make Chad do it," she joked, a glimmer of mischief in her eyes.

He winked, clearly ready to humor her. "I am." He thrust a broom and pan into Chad's reluctant hands. "I'll grab the trash bags from the office and return to clean up this mess."

"Thank you." Reena smiled appreciatively, grateful for his willingness to help.

"No problem at all," Bobby assured her. He leaned in conspiratorially. "And I'm going to charge him extra," he added with a grin.

Reena couldn't help but chuckle, shaking her head in agreement. "As you should."

Chad huffed a sigh, eyeing the mess around him and then glancing back at the broom and pan he now held. "I should have thought about this."

Part Two

It's All Fun and Games

Nasha's mind whirled in anger. All she saw was red in the parking lot, and she knew she needed to walk off before she said something she didn't mean. Her fist clenched at her sides as she stalked down the road. *Stupid ass boys and their pranks*, she huffed out a frustrated breath. *Of course, Reena thought it was funny.*

The further she walked, the more she realized she wasn't sure where she was going. Her head began to fog, and her knees suddenly hit the cold, hard ground. Nasha rolled onto her back with a low groan and stared at the starry night sky. Her vision blurred, and everything went dark.

My eyes fluttered open, staring at the late-night sky. Stars twinkled above me. It's been so long since I've seen stars or breathed in the cool, fresh air of the outside world. Being cooped up in the Clown Motel for the last ten years was rough. Only being able to breathe in the musk of that old run-down motel was not what I had anticipated, but now I'm free.

I should have known better than to get involved with a family steeped in voodoo and black magic. Sarah's pathetic family had woven dark spells that bound my soul to that grotesque, giant clown statue, now a relic in the middle of the motel's dimly lit lobby. A fucking perfect place to prey on a soul, but no one dared to touch me.

They gifted me to the motel's old owner, who seemed utterly uninterested in the officers' investigations into the strange occurrences surrounding the place.

The night I finally scared him off, I couldn't help but chuckle at the thought of his startled face when I had managed to move. When the new owner arrived, my lips curled into a smirk; he was blissfully oblivious to my presence—every flicker of the outdated neon sign outside. Every guest that left. Every chuckle heard through the night and every knock on the wall. I reveled in my hidden power, watching as he went about his business, completely unaware of the sinister forces at play within the motel's walls. I sat and waited for this perfect moment.

I rotated my neck and stretched out my back as I glanced down at the body I now inhabited and smiled. She was strong. Her mind fought me for two hours before she let me take over. It's like she knew, but I still won in the end. I stood from the ground and spun in circles with my arms stretched out. Laughing.

"Ah." I smiled. "Now, this feels good."

If only I knew what time of year it was and what kind of stores were around here. Hmmm. My index finger tapped my chin as I surveyed the empty desert. There has to be something. I skipped down the road, covered in a light layer of dirt, smiling until a small town had finally come into view. I wasn't sure what I was looking for, but it would be fun.

A rundown gas station light flickered as I skipped through the deserted parking lot. I rummaged through the pockets of the body I now inhabited and pulled out a small, worn-out wallet with a wad of cash. Perfect. My gaze snagged on her ID, Nasha Stone, 23. Damn, I'm gorgeous. My finger traced over the photo. Her kinky curls were in a fro, and her mocha skin was clear and flawless. High cheekbones and full lips. Shit! I turned myself on. I strolled into the store, the chime echoing in the small space. I snatched a bag of sour gummy worms and a tall can of Dr. Pepper from the shelf.

I giggled as my hand ran along the shelf, knocking off bags and bars of treats while going up to the counter. It's been far too long since I've been able to play. There was a collection of small pocket knives dangling from a rotating stand. I plucked the pretty pink one and slid it across the counter.

A guy with shaggy, dirty blonde hair stood behind the

counter. His green eyes flickered between me and the items on the counter. I smiled the best I could. This girl was hot. I bet I could flirt my way through anything. I was sexy, invincible. The last time I had possessed a body, I took on their wants, desires, and needs, but this girl was a jumbled mess between sexy, confident, and insecure. It wasn't body insecurity... hmmm... It was a relationship. I could taste it.

"Oh, this is going to be so much fun." I jumped up and down, clapping my hands with a wide smile.

His forehead scrunched. "Uh—What is?"

"That's for me to know." I grinned and gave him an unmistakable wink.

"Okay?" The guy behind the counter glared at me. "Total is ten bucks."

I pulled out the wallet and gave him the money he needed so that I could have my new items.

"Can I tell you something?" I bit my lip and leaned in.

His brows furrowed. "Sure?" He leaned in.

The cool knife bit into my hand. I flicked it open.

"I love your hair," I said, teasingly running a hand through it. I took a handful, pulling back his head a little so his neck was exposed over the counter.

"Feisty one, aren't you?" He chuckled. "Let's slow down here, babe."

"Only a little." I licked his neck up to his ear, then nibbled his lobe. "Sorry!" I kept a grip on his head, yanked it back, and shoved the knife into his jugular. His muscles tightened, and blood poured down his neck, dripping onto the counter. I held the knife there for several seconds before I slowly pulled it down and released his head from my grip. His eyes widened as he choked on blood, poorly attempting to hold the gash closed with his hands. "I really am sorry." I placed a kiss on his forehead.

His body slumped over the counter as a crimson pool of blood seeped from his neck.

I smeared my hand in his blood and spread it across his face, then wiped my hand on his shirt. "Yuck," I said as I snatched my blood-splattered drink and candy off the counter and shoved his body off. I glanced over at the man who lay on the floor, reached around the counter, grabbed the cash out of the register, shoved it into a brown bag with my items, and skipped out of the store.

The bag swung at my side as I skipped down the empty street. The lights flickered, and the cold nipped my skin, but I was free. The little town had a small strip of stores. A custom costume shop caught my eye, and my face lit up. There was something vaguely familiar as I approached the store, and two clown costumes came into view. One was red and white with colored dots, and the other was blue with colored dots.

I tried the door, and it didn't budge. I cupped my hands around my eyes and peered inside; no one was in there. I wonder what time it was. My hands immediately searched my pockets, and a slender, long box was in my back pocket. I pulled it out, and the screen lit up, displaying the time of midnight. The background was of her and a girl with long blonde hair with purple tips kissing.

You stay away from her!

"Ah, you're still here to play?"

This is my body, and I want it back!

Her presence pounded against the blockage in her mind, and I chuckled. "You're not that strong, sweetheart."

Get out of me, or I'll rip you to shreds.

"I can taste your anger, you know. The anger you hold toward the one on your phone screen."

Nasha's presence went dormant.

I cocked my head to the side and stared at my reflection in the glass before grabbing a handful of rocks scattered around the parking lot and chucking them at the window. The last rock hit the same spot as the one before cracking it ever so slightly. I walked up to the crack in the window and rammed my boot through it, shattering it completely. I clapped as I jumped up and down. Excitement I hadn't felt in years coursed its way through my new body.

The silky blue costume caressed my fingertips, and a taste of revenge hit my lips. Nasha sure was riled up when I took her over. The suit slipped off the hook, and I slid over her body. "Ah, this is satisfying." I smiled as I took in all the masks along the wall. My fingers skimmed each one as I admired them in passing. "Now, which one do we want?"

I stepped back and peered at the display wall, but none appealed to our inner desires. *Oh, Nasha, such a bougie babe.* The plastic crumpled to the floor as I opened the makeup box and painted my new face. I dipped the brush in the black paint and made a triangle above my eyes and below, then connected the bottom points to the corners of my mouth. With the red paint, I smudged it around the black and added red over her black lipstick. Above the tips of the triangle, I dotted two white circles and stepped away from the mirror.

"This just won't do." I tapped my chin. "Something is off." I scanned my body from head to toe. *Ahhh, it's the hair.* I split our kinky curls down the middle and put them into high pigtails. I clapped my hands and jumped up and down as I took in our reflection. "Now we are ready!"

Glass crunched under my boots as I stepped out of the store. The silk of the costume sashayed around my skin. Nasha had a mixture of feelings swirling within her: guilt and happiness. I smiled. She's darker than she wants, but she's enjoying this as much as I am.

I giggled and skipped toward the motel, shoveling the candy I had just gotten into my mouth. I wasn't sure how I knew it was back down this way, but I did. I was drawn to it. It was pulling me, or maybe Nasha was finally allowing me into her desires and leading me to find the ones she wanted to seek revenge on. Her pent-up anger fueled me; it was so potent it was bitter on my tongue. I cracked open the drink, the fizz sliding down my throat, a sensation I never thought I'd feel again.

Light fog rolled over while I was in the store, setting a low haze. The familiar deep red building with colorful dots came into view, and my heart thundered against my chest. I was ready to play. The back of the enormous clown sign sat way above the roof of the building. For ten years, I had been trapped in the main office. Watching people walk away and talk about the clown figurines and how creepy they were. The way they looked at me while I sat dormant in Willie the Clown, waiting for someone to touch me. Waiting for someone who had the same energy as me. Once Nasha brushed my cheek, I slid into her head and found she wasn't the sweet, close-off girl she appeared to be. I knew we would be the perfect match.

A man in the same blue suit as mine leaned against the wall, smoking a cigarette. I stood, watched, and waited. He ran a hand through his blonde hair before typing on his phone with one hand and slowly putting the lit cigarette between his full lips.

"Time to play, Nasha." I smiled, clutching the knife in my hand.

Nasha's presence slammed into me in full force, giving me a slight headache. I tried to push her back, but she wouldn't let me.

You can't do this! They are innocent people.

"Oh, but you are still so mad. I can taste it."

Friends get mad at friends sometimes. It's okay. I'll get over it.

My hand gripped the knife. "You will once I serve them the justice they *deserve*." The last word lingered in the air as I suppressed Nasha back into the cage she was so keen to escape.

The guy's name played on my lips, *Chad*. I cocked my head and smiled as I sized him up. Tall, lean, fit, he played a sport, football maybe? It was there, but I couldn't put my finger on it. I squatted behind a tumbleweed as a gust of wind blew through the flat grounds. I followed it toward the motel, sitting less than two yards from Chad.

A small gust of wind picked up, and his sandalwood cologne filled my senses. I bolted from behind the tumbleweed toward Chad, whose head still looked down as he typed away on his phone. His hand lifted the cigarette, bringing it to his mouth.

I slowed my pace and stood before him, keeping my knife in hand behind my back.

"Nasha?" he said, exhaling the smoke. "What are you doing in that costume?" he said through a chuckle. "Are you trying to get us back for messing with you?"

I shrugged, my fingers itching to kill him instantly, but this man was a fine specimen, and I sure liked to play.

"Maybe," I said, taking a deliberate step forward. "Or maybe I just want you."

His gaze widened as a grin spread across his face.

"What?" His eyes roamed my body before they darted away. "You're with Reena, dude."

I stepped even closer, closing the space between us. "And?"

He bit his lip and shook his head. "Fuck. This is wrong."

I giggled softly as I leaned into him, his sandalwood scent wrapping around me like a spell. Maybe Nasha's feelings were more complicated than I thought.

"Very," I teased, my breath mingling with his, daring him to make the move. Chad's gaze fell onto my lips; his head leaned forward, but I pulled back before we could touch.

His brows pulled as he looked down at me with a pinched expression at the last second as I drove the short, cool blade of the pocket knife into his stomach. His phone and cigarette clattered to the ground as his hands instinctively gripped my hand, holding the knife in place. I twisted the knife that was now submerged in his stomach before ripping it back out. Chad's blue eyes flickered up to mine as he let out a groan.

"Nasha?" He slumped back into the deep red-painted wall. "Why?"

I shrugged. "I just want to play." I smiled as I drove the knife back into his side. He groaned while I twisted it slowly and then dragged it to the left side of his body as he slid to the ground. I pulled out the knife, wiped his warm blood on my suit, and sat beside him. I picked up the cigarette and inhaled. The sweet taste of tobacco hit my taste buds, and I chuckled. It's been so long since I've had a drag or two.

Chad's hands were covered in blood as he clutched his stomach. His blue suit was turning red, and blood started to pool around us.

"Chad, man. You're making a mess. Do you need some help?" I flicked the cigarette away from me into the dirt field.

He shook his head as his hands fell to his side.

"Giving up so easy. I thought you'd have more fight than that." I climbed onto his lap and straddled him, fisting a hand into his soft blonde hair. I yanked his head to the side to expose his neck. Sandalwood and metal lingered between us. I placed a gentle kiss on his neck before flicking out my tongue and running it up his neck to his ear, sucking on it.

Chad let out a small groan but didn't move.

I placed small kisses from his lobe to his mouth before savoring his tobacco-filled kiss. My hands gripped his cheeks before placing one last kiss on those full lips. I stood and kicked him in the head. His body thudded against the gravel, and his eyes stared blankly ahead as his blood surrounded his body.

His phone vibrated on the ground, the screen flashing white as I picked it up.

Bryce: Hey man, where are you?

Me: Out back smoking a cig
Bryce: The owner left a broom and bucket for you haha
Me: I'll be right there

Bryce sent a thumbs up as I tossed the phone back into Chad's lap.

Dim lights lit the outside of each door down the open hall. The parking lot only had one beat-up vehicle that the girl I now possessed arrived in. I knew the motel's owner, Bobby, lived upstairs as I strolled toward the only room with a broom, dustpan, and bucket outside. My hands traced the wooden walls as I stopped outside of the room. My eyes flickered to the ceiling as footsteps creaked above me. It may be time for Bobby to pay the price. All the years, I sat and stared at that god-awful front office. All the years, I gave signs there was life within his precious life-like doll that he chose to ignore, thinking it was some residual haunting because some paranormal investigators told him that years ago. I could have been freed. I could have lived my whole life and moved on. *Could I move on? Or was I stuck here?*

A smile crept across my face. *Did I truly want to move on?* I loved to play games. I glanced down at the broom and pan. The mess could wait. Glass crunched under my shoes as I fixated on the noise upstairs. Music played so lightly that I couldn't distinguish what was playing as I ascended the creaky wooden steps to the second floor.

The footsteps and music grew louder as I quickly but

quietly walked across the balcony floor. He left a window open, and white curtains fluttered in the breeze. I squatted and peeked through the old window. He had the television on a channel that played today's greatest hits as he moved around the kitchen, opening cupboards and pulling out spices. Whatever he was cooking up smelled delicious. I licked my lips.

Bob swayed his hips as he sprinkled spice on the meat in the pan, then swiped his forearm over his sweaty bronze forehead, slightly moving his curly black hair to the side. He smiled as he danced alone, seemingly in peace with what he was doing. *Was a life alone in this motel enough for him? If so, how? Why? Was his sufficient obsession enough to keep him happy?* Spending time with all these figurines that are given to him. People talk to him about these items he collected over the years as if this is all life offers.

My hand gripped the knife, my knuckles whitening as I watched him cook. Time passed as he plated his food and sat on his old couch, flipping through the channels until he landed on Discovery. The plate of food sat perched on top of his round belly. In some ways, this man intrigued me. His life was simple. His desires were unpretentious. It was as if this was all he ever needed.

He ate his plate slowly as he watched the television and began to drift off. His snoring woke him up every so often. More time went by as I sat crouched under the window. His head fell to the side, his plate slid off his body onto the couch, and he didn't wake up this time. The window squealed as I pushed it open the rest of the way and slowly crept in. My mouth watered at the aroma of his dinner.

Strolling into the kitchen, I spotted a gleaming fork resting beside the pan on the stovetop. Without a second thought, I grabbed it and dove into the delicious chaos within. The rich and flavorful seasoned hamburger meat melted deliciously on my tongue, a symphony of spices dancing in my mouth.

"Damn, this man can cook," I murmured, barely able to contain my appreciation. My posture slumped slightly as I leaned over the pan, eagerly shoveling forkful after forkful into my mouth, the warm meat instantly satisfying my hunger. I couldn't remember the last time I had eaten, not that I needed to, but food was one thing I'd never give up.

I finally glanced around as I indulged and noticed the spread before me. A steaming mound of perfectly cooked noodles was nestled beside the pan, glistening with a drizzle of olive oil and scattered herbs. A golden, crusty loaf of garlic bread sat enticingly on a nearby plate, its rich aroma wafting through the air. It was a feast in the making, but the hamburger meat had captured my full attention.

I selected a warm slice of freshly baked bread, feeling its inviting softness as I brought it closer. As I took a hearty bite, the delicate texture yielded quickly, melting pleasantly on my tongue. Relishing the moment, I licked my fingers clean, savoring every last crumb, before reaching for a nearby napkin to discreetly wipe away any remnants of the indulgence. It's been so long since I've had a proper meal that my stomach was extended.

A floorboard creaked ominously behind me, a sound that sliced through the tense silence of the dimly lit room. I turned sharply, my heart racing, to find Bob cautiously approaching his front door. The corners of his ordinarily cheerful face were twisted in terror, his brown eyes wide and frantically scanning his surroundings. A glistening sheen of sweat gathered on his brow, catching the flickering light from the nearby lamp, and I could see his fingertips tremble as they neared the doorknob.

"Now, now, Bobby, you don't want to do that," I said, my voice smooth yet laced with a threatening undertone. I brandished the small blade of my pocket knife, its edge glinting menacingly in the low light. "Sit down like a good boy." I gestured with the knife, directing his attention firmly to the worn couch that sat against the wall, its fabric fraying at the seams.

Bob's fear-ridden eyes darted between the door, which represented escape, and the couch, symbolizing compliance. I could almost hear the frantic pounding of his heart as he weighed his options, and the tension thickened in the air around us.

I folded my arms casually, stifling a yawn to feign disinterest, but I was fully engaged inside. "Are we going to do this the hard way?" I asked a grin creeping across my face that didn't quite reach my eyes. I found the prospect amusing; confrontation was never truly a bother for me. Still, a part of me would prefer it if Nasha's friends hadn't caught wind of my presence here just yet. After all, I had a special plan for them, one that demanded a bit of patience.

His hand dropped slowly, a clear sign of defeat. "Look, I don't want any problems."

Bobby glanced around his living room one last time, taking in the clutter of everyday life—the scattered magazines on the coffee table, the half-drunk cup of cold coffee, and the muted colors of the worn-out sofa. As he walked toward the couch, his head hung low, and his shoulders drooped forward. "I apologize for the prank. I didn't think it'd get that far." He sniffled.

I couldn't wait any longer; the itch to feel the coolness of this small blade stick into him as smoothly as butter overcame me. I pranced up to him and stabbed him directly below his right shoulder blade. The blade stuck out of his back as I giggled, and he howled in agony. I kicked the back of his leg. His leg buckled, and down he went.

"It's not about the fucking prank, Bobby," I spat as I sat on him. "You never noticed me!" I plucked out the knife and plunged it back into him as he kicked and fought. "You let me sit for ten fucking years while everyone looked at me."

"I'm sorry!" He cried. "I can't feel my legs."

"Oh, poor Bobby," I said as I skipped into the kitchen

and grabbed the wooden knife block off the cluttered counter from tonight's dinner. Bob was still lying on the ground, his hand trying to reach the knife in his back but failing miserably. I yanked it from his back. He let out a deep, relieving breath before it hitched again, and he let out an agonizing cry.

"Please stop!" He howled.

I rolled my eyes, unable to keep the annoyance to myself. "It'll be over before you know it." I grabbed a knife from the block and straddled his back, sliding it in near his spine.

"What do you want?" He whimpered, his face reddened and wet as tears streaked his cheeks.

I grabbed another knife, sticking it into his back. "The taste of your blood."

He gasped.

"I sat by your side for over ten years. I know all about you." I pushed on the knife, bones cracking underneath the weight. "You've owned this place for years now, walking past me as if I didn't exist while I sat on display for everyone to stare at. As if I was a circus clown. *Oh, Silly Willy is so life-like,*" I said tauntingly. "And you never knew I was in there. I pleaded and talked to you for years, and you've never heard me, did you?"

The one eye I could see darted around as his face smushed into the wooden floor. "I—I didn't."

"That's all I needed to know." I twisted the knife by his

spine, and his limbs fell limp by his side, all the tension gone. He was paralyzed.

"I'm sorry. Please, I can't feel my body. Please—"

I grabbed the last knife he had in the wooden block, fisted my hand in his hair, lifted his head, and slowly slid the blade across his throat. Bob gurgled as I dropped his head—deep red pooled around his upper body.

"I love it when people beg." I stood from his now lifeless body.

Nasha's rage and fear bubbled inside me as she watched everything I did with absolutely no control. *Keep begging, love. I relish it.*

Fuck you, she spat.

My mouth curled up. "Let's go meet your friends." I rubbed my hands together as the anticipation within me built. "Now, let's see if he has anything useful for us."

Each corner overflowed with the remnants of his life as he seemed to gather an endless array of belongings over time. I vividly recall when he brought in another batch of colorful clowns, their painted faces and brightly patterned outfits contrasting sharply with the dull beige walls of the lobby.

It wasn't just the clowns; every week, it felt like he was hauling up armfuls of discarded treasures—old record players with their worn-out turntables, stacks of yellowing magazines long forgotten, and an assortment of trinkets he believed were collectibles but were in reality, little more than useless clutter. The hallway often echoed with his footsteps as he navigated through the maze of his own making, each item telling a story yet collectively forming a chaotic tapestry that defined his living quarters.

I discovered a baseball bat lying idly beside his bed, its smooth wood cool against my fingers as I wrapped my hands around its handle. It felt surprisingly light, effortlessly swinging through the air with a satisfying whoosh. As I positioned it against my shoulder, I glanced back at his still form, lifeless eyes wide open and fixed on me, a beautiful reminder of what had just transpired. With force, I retrieved my small pocket knife from his body, its blade glinting faintly in the dim light. I slipped it into my pocket, but the night wasn't over just yet.

The warm night air brushed against my skin as I quietly shut the door behind me. Now that Chad and Bobby were taken care of, it was time to rip apart those siblings and make them watch while no one was around to help them. Their pleas were going to be of no use. I smiled as my footsteps creaked down the wooden steps, and the bat resting on my shoulder bumped around.

That little beat-up car still sat outside the deserted motel. The welcome sign flickered erratically in the front window. The night sky was full of stars twinkling above. I stopped two doors from room 107, staring at the window's reflection. My smile widened. My paint was smudged, and blood splattered across my neck, face, and hai

r.

I giddily walked toward Reena and her brother Bryce's room, stopping short when the door swung open.

Reena poked her head out, staring the other way. "Chad! Are you done smoking?"

My hand covered my mouth as I giggled.

"Chad?" Reena stepped out of the room.

My other hand tightened on the bat.

"Chad?" She stepped closer to the side of the building. "You better not be fucking around."

I went to step forward, but my body wouldn't move. My eyes darted around as my mouth wouldn't open. My fingers couldn't tap the bat, and my legs were cemented.

How's it feel to not be in control, motherfucker? Nasha spat as she rattled the cage.

"I will win this fight." I managed to bite out.

Over my dead body.

"Do you love her?" I slowly smacked my lips as I got my movement back.

I'm not telling you.

"You don't need to. I can taste it." I licked my lips as the bitter love danced across them.

I wiggled my fingers and toes as I shoved Nasha's annoying presence down. The coolness of the knob nipped the palm of my hand as I turned the handle and stepped into the room beside them.

"Reena?" The familiar voice of her brother called out.

"Is Chad—"

I stepped from the room, swinging the bat down with a loud crack across his skull. He loudly grunted as he kneeled on the floor, rubbing the back of his head. "Dude, what the—"

The bat came back down onto his head, and his body collapsed onto the floor.

Without a chance to look up, a body clashed with mine, landing on top of me. A beautiful petite blonde with purple tips was straddling me. Her eyes narrowed. Reena was fuming.

"What the fuck are you doing, Nasha?" Her arm cocked back, her fist tightened.

As much as I liked her sitting on my lap, I didn't like being on the bottom. I threw my hips up, and Reena toppled over as I stood, baseball bat in hand.

"Come on. You seriously can't be that mad over a prank, babe." As she stood, her eyes darted nervously between me and her brother, who lay groaning on the ground. Reena took a tentative step closer, her body tense and rigid as if bracing for an impact. "Why are you dressed like that? Where did all this blood come from, Nasha?" The vein on her forehead throbbed, pulsing in rhythm with the rapid beat of her heart. I could see the uncertainty clouding her gaze, mingling with concern as she tried to process the chaotic scene unfolding around us.

As I stood there, something shifted within me, a sensation that softened the tension I had been holding. My knuckles, once rigid around the smooth grip of the bat, started to relax as I felt a warmth spreading through me. I watched Reena cautiously approaching, her movements deliberate and unhurried, as if trying to navigate a fragile moment. Like a clear summer sky, her light blue eyes held my gaze with unwavering intensity, searching for understanding and perhaps a glimmer of reassurance. In that suspended moment, the world around us seemed to fade away, leaving only her and the fragile connection we were beginning to forge.

Her small, soft hand gently rested on my upper arm, radiating warmth through the colorful fabric of my clown suit. I couldn't help but smile—truly smile. The warmth of her touch and the innocence of her gesture made my heart swell. I frowned. This wasn't me. I was feeling Nasha's feelings, and before I could react, the bat was ripped out of my hands.

"Reena, run!" The words escaped my lips before I could fully process what was happening, and as if on instinct, I pushed her back with all my strength. Panic coursed through my veins, and I could barely articulate the fear that gripped me. "It's not me. There's something—"

Suddenly, a deafening crack echoed through the air, cutting through the chaos like a knife. Instantly, a jarring wave of agony surged through my skull, sharp and unforgiving, as if a million thorns had punctured my mind.

My vision blurred, and I stumbled forward, disoriented, struggling to keep my balance while the world around me spun wildly.

"Run!!" Bryce shouted as his leg cocked back before he swung his leg full force, kicking me in the stomach and knocking the air from my lungs.

Reena gasped at the action her brother took upon her lover before she turned her back and darted toward her car. Bryce dropped the bat and tried to take off, but I gripped his leg, causing him to stumble. My grip was firm, and he couldn't shake me off.

The car door slammed shut, and the locks clicked. Reena hit the horn repeatedly, screaming, 'Come on, Bryce!' and trying to draw attention to us this early in the morning in a lonely town.

I pulled the knife from my pocket, slicing his achilles, the thickest tendon in the human body, before shoving the knife into his calf. Bryce let out a roar of pain as he hit the cement. I stood, shaking the wave of agony that still pulsed through my skull.

Tears cascaded down Reena's cheeks, mingling with the remnants of her thick black eyeliner, which now formed dark streaks that framed her face. Her nose was bright red, starkly contrasting to her pale skin, and her throat was raw from calling out for her brother, her voice hoarse and strained. Desperation laced her cries, each scream echoing in the heavy silence, amplifying the anguish that consumed her.

My plan had gone to shit, and anger bubbled through me. I grabbed Bryce by his hair and lifted him upright, his face turned toward his sister.

"Nasha, it was only a joke," he pleaded.

I laughed. "Nasha's no longer in charge."

His face fell flat. Reena stopped honking the car horn. Her cries went silent as I lifted my knife in the air before it came down, stabbing Bryce in the center of his throat—blood spurt out of his mouth. A loud cry ripped through the air. My hand sawed back and forth as my other hand gripped his hair tightly. Bryce sputtered and gurgled one last time before the rest of the tension in his body left him and hit the ground with a thud.

I held up his head and kissed his cheek. Blood dripped from his open mouth, and his eyes stared lifelessly into Reena's. Reena's red, puffy eyes never left mine as she backed out of the Clown Motel's parking lot. Her face was void of all emotion as she slowly rolled away from the scene.

"You were supposed to die!" I bellowed, but my anger subsided as a laugh escaped my throat.

You lost at your own game.

"Did I?" I tapped my finger on my chin. "Reena will never forgive you. You killed her bro—"

No, that was you!

"But it was your body. Your face." I chuckled. "Your face

is all over the gas station cameras. Your fingerprints are all over the weapons and motel. When I leave your body and find my next victim, your life will be ruined, and I'll be running around having fun."

Nasha didn't respond, but the taste of disappointment and realization flooded my veins. It was satisfying. Her cage went quiet. Her fight was gone. I had won, after all.

"Now, let's go have more fun." I smirked as I stepped over Bryce's headless body.

Part Three

I Promise I'll Find You

It has now been eleven long, agonizing months since the horrific incident at the Clown Motel, a time that feels like an eternity since my brother was taken from me by Nasha—eleven months filled with a heavy weight of grief and unanswered questions. As the weeks turned into months, the days began to blur together, marked only by endless interviews with the police, each one more draining than the last.

The investigators were adamant that all the collected evidence pointed clearly to Nasha as the prime suspect. Yet, despite their extensive efforts, she seemed to have vanished without a trace, leaving no clues behind. I repeated, time and again, what I had witnessed during that harrowing evening—the chilling words she spoke just before everything changed.

The last haunting exchange my brother, Bryce, had with her echoed in my mind: "Nasha's no longer in charge," she had told him with an unsettling calmness, suggesting something sinister lurking beneath the surface. It felt like a part of her had been consumed by something darker that had taken control, and I was left powerless to save my brother from it. The agony of knowing she is still out there, beyond reach, gnaws at me with each passing day.

The walls of my bedroom, which once proudly displayed vibrant posters of boy bands and legendary rock stars, now presented a chilling collage of yellowing newspaper clippings and printed internet articles chronicling the infamous Clown Motel Murders. A heavy sense of unease hung in the air as I gazed at the stark contrast between my youthful dreams and this grim fixation. I was painfully aware she was not in control of her actions, yet the true force behind everything remained elusive and vague—an enigma I felt compelled to unravel.

I had watched the recording of that day to retrace our steps over and over again from the time we arrived to the time I left my brother's lifeless body on the cold ground next to his murderer. The one image my mind snagged onto was Nasha touching Willie's life-like doll. The way she shuddered when she did. The way she seemed to fight herself as she attacked Bryce. She told me to run before her eyes returned to a blank stare, the fear that was there replaced with emptiness.

It was finally time to head back to the Clown Motel and confront the mystery that had haunted me for so long. A sense of urgency washed over me as I looked around my dimly lit room. I began to tear down the news clippings and printed articles that cluttered my walls, remnants of a desperate attempt to piece together what had transpired. Each yellowed page felt weighty with misinformation, filled with sensational headlines and half-truths that led me nowhere.

The media had spun their narratives to comfort an audience craving coherence in chaos. Still, the stories were empty fabrications for those directly intertwined in this dark web. I could feel the frustration boiling within me as I crumpled the pages in my hands, knowing all too well that these stories trivialized the pain and confusion of those who indeed suffered. It was time to dig deeper, to uncover the truth buried beneath the circus of lies.

Tears streaked down my face as I sat on my bed. Crumbled papers littered the floor. I pulled my laptop onto my lap and opened the search engine.

Can you trap an evil entity?

Hundreds of articles flooded my screen. My eyes repeatedly scanned the page from left to right until the words blurred. The phrase 'how to tie an entity to an object' caught my eye.

Exorcism. Salt. Iron. Devil's Circle.

My eyes narrowed in on the words. My mouse scrolled

the article before I found myself on a dark webpage with hundreds of instructions on exorcising a demon or entity, then binding it to an object and keeping it bound. I grabbed a notebook from my nightstand, slid the pen out of the rings, and wrote down everything. Step by step. I wasn't even sure this was something I could do on my own, and I wasn't even sure where Nasha was now, but as the one-year mark approached, nothing was stopping me from figuring it out.

As if on cue, just one week before the anniversary of the Clown Motel Murders, Nasha was spotted two states away, her presence electrifying the airwaves. News outlets plastered her image across screens and newspapers, her haunting eyes staring back at a frightened public. In the wake of her sighting, a tragic scene unfolded at a lonely gas station, where life was snuffed out far too soon. It was as predictable as the ticking of a clock. The first victim, a hardworking gas station attendant, fell prey to the malevolent shadow that seemed to follow Nasha eerily close to the infamous Clown Motel.

I packed a duffle bag of clothes and necessities. Determination took over as I tossed the bags I had packed for the last three weeks into the trunk. Duffle bags full of paint, iron, salt, and a doll in hopes I could save Nasha from whatever had a hold of her—if something had a hold of her. I knew in my gut she wouldn't do the things that were done, but my heart fought me. She'd been acting differently the weeks leading up to the Clown Motel, and half of me wondered if it was her, so she snapped. After all, everyone has a breaking point.

My trunk slammed shut as I packed the last of my stuff into my car. I slid into the driver's seat and let out an exaggerated sigh. Frustration, hurt, and confusion bubbled inside me. It was as if I was preparing for war. I survived the first time. Would I survive *this one*?

Good evening, 97.8! We are informing you that a significant downpour is forecasted for Montana. Please make sure to stay warm and drive safely. Now—Reena turned off the radio, her thoughts racing as she entered Montana. Her windshield wipers were on high, but she could barely keep up with the downpour. She glanced at her phone mounted on the dash. Ten minutes until she got to her hotel. Nerves shot through her body.

Reena had anticipated this moment for a year, and her heart thrummed with hope and determination. For the last month, she immersed herself in the intricate study of new languages, each word she learned swirling around her like a protective shield. Her nights were filled with research into gruesome murders, each case a chilling echo of the horrific fates that befell Chad, Bobby, and Bryce.

During her investigations, she unearthed the dark legacy of a man named Amon Bellinor—an embodiment of pure malevolence. He killed for sheer amusement, without any discernible motive compelling his brutal actions. His twisted reign of terror came to an end in Montana during the 1800s, yet Reena felt an unsettling certainty that he had returned to the very ground that once bore witness to his atrocities.

As she delved deeper into Amon's haunting past, Reena became increasingly convinced that he was the malevolent force responsible for possessing Nasha. Over the past eleven months, she meticulously gathered everything needed to confront this evil, not only for Nasha's sake but for all the souls devastated by Amon's insatiable thirst for violence. The time had come to end this horror cycle once and for all.

The last little piece of information she needed was only recently revealed, and she was shocked she could get all the little pieces required for this. Now, she needed to draw him in and trap him, which was the only part of this plan she wasn't sure how to execute. The hotel's parking lot was filled with cars and people walking about. A little of the tension Reena was feeling released from her shoulders. One thing she knew was he loved secluded areas.

Reena threw her cross-body bag over her shoulder as she clicked the locks into place, ensuring her belongings were secure before she stepped towards the towering Soft Park Hotel. The hotel loomed before her, gracefully stretching five stories high, its exterior a soothing light blue that reflected the morning sky.

As Reena entered, she was greeted by a lively scene in the

main lobby. The air was filled with the murmur of voices and the clatter of wheeled luggage as guests checked in and out. After a moment of scanning the crowded space, she grabbed a sturdy lobby cart, its metal frame gleaming under the overhead lights. The wheels shook as she returned to her car and meticulously loaded the cart with various bags: four duffle bags in multiple colors, each brimming with her essentials and a sleek backpack perched on top. It was a lot for just a three-day stay, but it was precisely what she needed to feel prepared and at home.

The elevator creaked and groaned as it ascended, packed tightly with guests hurrying to their destinations. She stood near the back, her lobby cart shuddering slightly as the doors opened on the fourth floor. With a firm grip on her cart, she navigated through the crowd, feeling the gentle buzz of anticipation as she neared the door to her room. She reached the door, pulled out her key card, and slid it into the electronic lock with a satisfying beep. She pushed her cart inside as the lock clicked and the door eased open. The soft thud of the door shutting echoed in the spacious room.

Once she locked the door behind her, she took in her surroundings. The hotel room blended modern elegance and comfort, featuring a sumptuous king-size bed draped in crisp white linens and adorned with plush pillows. On either side of the bed stood matching nightstands, each equipped with a lamp. A substantial dresser held a large flat-screen TV facing the bed. The balcony beckoned her with its inviting presence, adorned with a small, round table and two sturdy chairs, perfect for sipping coffee while enjoying the view outside. A view she hoped she'd be able to enjoy with Nasha once this was all over.

To her right, the bathroom door swung open to reveal a sanctuary of relaxation, complete with a deep soaking tub and a separate glass-enclosed shower. The room was alive with countless details, including the inviting aroma of clean linens and the soft sounds of the city below.

Reena quickly grabbed her worn backpack and flopped down onto the hotel bed. She pulled out her sleek laptop and powered it on, the screen illuminating her determined expression as she connected to the hotel's sluggish wifi. With a few swift clicks, she typed in 'secluded areas in Montana,' and her heart raced.

Three locations caught her eye as the search results populated, but one stood out above the rest. It was just an hour's drive from the gas station where the gruesome murder had taken place recently, a chilling reminder of what was to be done. The location was described as a quaint bed and breakfast in a more remote part of town.

Curiosity piqued, Reena zoomed in on the map, her fingers trembling slightly as she scrolled over the details. The bed and breakfast was perched on the outskirts, bordered by thick woods and rolling hills, far removed from the small downtown strip bustling with tourists. This isolated retreat offered the perfect cover. Her instincts told her that this was where he had to hide, and the distance was a mere hour away—a short drive for someone seeking answers. The hunt was on, and she prepared to set out with a resolve forged by desperation.

Reena jumped off the bed, slipped out of her clothes, and headed for the shower. The warm water cascaded down her head and body. Steam filled the air as she stepped out—a soft towel wrapped around her body. Reena clutched the countertop and looked into the mirror. The bags under her eyes were a year's worth of no sleep.

"Tonight's the night, motherfucker." Reena pushed off the cool surface of the granite. She slipped into her black jeans, the fabric hugging her legs snugly, and reached for a fitted white tank top that accentuated her toned arms. Her combat boots were scuffed but sturdy as she laced them tightly, ready for whatever lay ahead.

Reena clasped iron bracelets around her wrists, each a small weight that grounded her in the moment. Around her neck, she secured a pendant holding holy water encased in iron. Though Reena had never believed in the efficacy of such relics, the night felt charged with an unspoken tension, and she was compelled to take every precaution. Desperate times call for desperate measures, and tonight, she was ready to embrace that truth.

Was everything Nasha's *doing*, or did Amon Bellinor

possess her?

The charming bed and breakfast was just four miles from the iconic Welcome to Choteau sign. The establishment was housed in an old, two-story Victorian home with a full wrap-around porch. Although the white paint was peeling in places, revealing the weathered wood beneath, the blue trim and roof gave the building a fresh and inviting touch, hinting at recent renovations.

As Reena pulled into the small gravel lot, she noticed two cars parked side by side—perhaps fellow travelers enjoying the quaint retreat. She chose to park toward the back of the lot, where dappled sunlight filtered through the surrounding trees, casting playful shadows on the ground.

She grabbed the two duffle bags from her back seat and headed across the parking lot. The front entrance had a small check-in and check-out table. Two rooms branched off from the entryway: a cute dining room with a long table and dim lighting and the living room with a huge sectional couch, a coffee table, and a TV mounted to the wall with a shelf underneath for the DVD player and remotes.

"Hello?" Reena called out.

A short older woman stepped out of another room beyond the living room, her white hair swaying above her shoulders.

"Hello, Dear. What can I help you with?"

Reena shifted the heavy duffle bag on her shoulder.

"I was wondering if you have any rooms available for tonight."

"I do," she said, removing and cleaning her glasses as she stepped behind the small table. "I have one more room. Can you sign in here, please?" She slid over a notebook and pen.

Reena grabbed the pen and scanned the names of the individuals staying there. Amanda Bellamy ... A.B. *Amon Bellinor.* Two nights ago, one person checked in under that name in room 201. Then, it looked like a group of friends had checked into the other rooms, the two cars she saw outside in the parking lot. He was going after another group of friends. *Did this mean he was going to possess another?*

She signed underneath the last name and dated it before sliding it back to the lady.

"Here is your room key. I'll take you up."

Reena shifted the bags once more and smiled. "Thank you."

The kitchen was next to the stairs. It was small, but the aroma wafting through it made Reena's mouth water. Photos of the lady and a man with what Reena assumed to be her guest lined the wall, along with pictures of her and the man hiking and other traveling pictures. This bed and breakfast was quite homey.

"My name is Eleanor, by the way," she said over her shoulder.

"Reena."

"What brings you to Choteau?"

Reena bit her lip as she glanced around the opening at the door numbers. "I like to sightsee."

Eleanor stopped outside the room labeled 200. "Here you are," she smiled. "If you like sightseeing, you should check out the Foxtail Trail. It stops at a clearing from which you can see the whole town." She held out the key to the door.

"I'll check it out. Thanks, Eleanor." Reena opened the door, dropping the bags against the wooden floor.

She let out a sigh of relief. "Time to get to work."

Reena carefully shifted the small, full bed to the side, revealing the worn wooden floor beneath. She knelt and pulled back the rug, its fabric rough against her fingertips. With a determined expression, she turned to her duffle bag, unzipping it swiftly, the zipper's teeth clicking audibly in the quiet room.

Reaching the bag's depths, her fingers brushed against the cool metal can containing her paint. She retrieved it, and the weight of the paint was reassuring in her hands. With a satisfying pop, she twisted off the lid. A strong, pungent odor of fresh paint wafted up as she dipped her brush into the vibrant red liquid, the bristles soaking up the color.

With each stroke, she began to outline the devil's circle on the bare wooden floor, the bright red contrasting sharply against the muted tones of the room. The lines were sharp and precise, reflecting the focused intent behind her actions. She meticulously painted intricate sigils within the circle, each infused with purpose.

A glossy sheen settled over the surface as the paint began to dry, glinting in the dim light. Reena's mind raced with anticipation as she turned her attention to a small, unsettling doll resting in the depths of her bag. Its porcelain skin looked pale and eerie, while its stitched mouth and mismatched eyes gave it an otherworldly presence—perfect for what she had planned. She picked it up, feeling the chill of its surface, and prepared to place it in the center of her newly painted creation. Her heart beat faster.

Reena carefully extracted a rusted piece of iron wire from a small pouch. She retrieved an ornate, weathered box, its surface etched with intricate patterns that hinted at its age and significance. Finally, she reached for a crinkled bag of salt, its contents spilling slightly at the edges, a reminder of the precautions she was preparing to take. With deliberate movements, she placed each item into the deep confines of the dresser drawer, organizing them with a sense of purpose.

As she stepped back, Reena shook her hands to release the tension within her, feeling the flutter of anxiety in her chest. She closed her eyes briefly, inhaling deeply and exhaling slowly, allowing the rhythm of her breath to calm her racing thoughts. Turning her gaze toward the window, she observed the sky painted in hues of orange and purple, the sun dipping low on the horizon. The day's warmth was fading. It was almost time.

Reena grabbed her journal and tore a piece of paper from it—r*oom 200. We have unfinished business.* She folded the paper and placed it in her back pocket.

The paint had dried to a smooth finish, glistening faintly in the dim light. Reena carefully placed the rug over the intricate patterns of the devil's circle she had painstakingly painted on the wooden floor. Her heart raced as she repositioned the bed, ensuring it blocked the circle from view. All she needed was for him to step into that trap, and then she could finally bind him there.

"I can do this," she whispered to herself, trying to quell the anxiety gnawing at her. With determination fueling her, she grabbed her worn duffle bags, their fabric frayed from years of use, and shoved them beneath the bed hurriedly. The symbols and incantations she had scribbled in her journal were her greatest hope; they contained the powerful phrases needed to exorcise the demon from Nasha.

Reena's brow furrowed as she recalled the countless nights she had spent hunched over her desk, her fingers dancing over the pages as she studied the ancient Latin phrases she had stumbled upon on a website promising authentic knowledge of the occult. She hoped fervently that it was not a mere hoax; after all, time was running out.

In all her research, she had uncovered grim possibilities. If a demon had truly possessed Nasha, it was likely that her girlfriend was trapped in her own body, fighting to break free from a malevolent force that had taken hold. The alternative haunted Reena's mind—that perhaps Nasha had already perished, her soul lost to this world while a dark entity masqueraded in her flesh. The only answer, the only way to uncover the truth, was to confront the demon and force it out of her beloved. Determined, Reena collected her thoughts, steeling herself for the battle ahead.

"Please don't let it be Nasha," Reena whispered to herself, her breath catching in her throat. She grasped the cold, tarnished doorknob with a shaky hand and slowly turned it, letting the creaky door groan open. The floorboards beneath her creaked softly, betraying her cautious steps, and she strained to listen for any sounds of Nasha in the dimly lit hallway. An unsettling silence surrounded her, amplifying her anxiety. They could be lurking nearby, preparing to strike, or worse, lying in wait, ready to ambush the friends staying here, like a predator stalking its prey.

A shiver ran down her spine as she carefully slipped the folded note under the door, her heart pounding. Like a thief in the night, she retreated to her room, the door clicking shut behind her. Alone in her sanctuary, she paced frantically, the shadows flickering around her as she tried to collect her thoughts. Finally, she sank onto her bed, her fingers brushing against the dresser, feeling the calm surface of her hidden objects, ready for whatever might come next. The weight of anticipation hung heavy as she prepared for the unknown.

The bracelets around Reena's wrist chimed together as she absentmindedly twiddled her fingers. The sun had retreated beyond the horizon, casting a deep indigo hue across the sky. A lively buzz of chatter reverberated like distant music. Outside her door, unsteady footsteps stumbled across the floor, their unpredictable rhythm punctuated by hushed whispers and suppressed giggles that danced on the edges of the air. Shadows flickered and swayed under her door, forming dark silhouettes that hinted at the presence of unseen revelers just beyond her room.

Reena sprang from the cozy bed, her heart racing as she swiftly activated the camera concealed behind the television next to the dusty DVD player. The device appeared innocuous, blending seamlessly into the room's decor, yet she knew its true purpose. With a furtive glance toward her door, she hurriedly plopped back onto the bed, the soft quilt crumpling beneath her. A swirl of uncertainty filled her mind, but one thing was clear—she needed to capture whatever unfolded next, desperate for evidence of the events to come.

"Night, Amanda!" a girl's voice called out.

"Night." Nasha's voice filled the air, and Reena's throat constricted.

Amanda Bellamy. A.B. He thought he was slick, using Nasha as a puppet. The air was thick with tension, and Reena could feel it coiling around her like a tight band. Every fiber of her being urged her to rise from her seat, to confront the game unfolding before her, but she remained rooted in place. She needed Nasha to come to her and trap her within the circle. She needed to piss her off to get close enough to attack her. The sound of doors creaking open and slamming shut echoed around her, yet Reena couldn't discern if Nasha had stepped through her threshold until her door swung wide open, revealing the shadows beyond.

The door slammed shut, echoing in the silence and extinguishing the warm glow behind the figure standing there. Nasha lingered in the doorway, a mere shadow of her former self. Once vibrant and full of life, she appeared frail, her body having lost its healthy weight. Her once-luscious, kinky curls hung in disarray, each strand a testament to neglect. The natural shine of her light mocha skin had dulled, leaving it parched and lifeless.

Her full lips, once expressive and inviting, appeared chapped and thin, and her high cheekbones now cast deep shadows across her face as if the weight of her sorrow had pushed them in. Nasha's eyes, usually bright and warm, seemed dim, betraying a struggle that might signal a serious illness or a slow deterioration.

Reena's heart ached at the sight, her anger simmering dangerously close to the surface, just as it had the night her brother was so cruelly taken from her. She choked back tears, torn between the desperate need to confront Nasha and the overwhelming anger to kill her.

Nasha took a step forward, her eyes narrowing. "Looking to join your brother?"

"No. I want my girlfriend back." Reena's fist clenched.

Nasha's eyes scanned the room, a smirk pulling at her lips as her hand slid down the dresser. "And what if I told you she's no longer here?"

Her back straightened. It was *true*. Nasha had nothing to do with this.

"How did you do it?" She folded her arms, trying to play it cool.

Her head cocked to the side. "Take over this voluptuous body?" She snickered. "It was easy. She touched the doll. I could taste her emotions. They are strong, and I latched on like a baby wanting milk. Though, she did put up a good fight. I won in the end."

"Fuck you, Amon Bellinor," Reena spat.

Nasha took another step forward, her hand reaching for her back pocket. Her eyes darkened as she lunged toward Reena and pressed a knife against her throat. "Someone did their homework," she hissed.

Amon was the one controlling Nasha, the one who had killed her brother. She had been waiting for this moment, and her blood boiled with vengeance. Her fingers closed around the bottom of the knife. She started to turn the blade toward Nasha, their hands shaking as they fought, and she plunged it into his shoulder. He dropped the knife and stumbled back, clutching his wound. Reena kicked him in the chest, sending him sprawling onto the floor.

"Oh, I did more than my homework." Reena glanced toward the ground.

Nasha's eyes followed before they flickered back up. "You think you're so fucking smart. Coming here and challenging me." She chuckled. "Time to meet your brother."

She charged Reena, wrapping her hands around her neck, her fingers digging into her throat. Reena fought back, her fingers clawing at his arm, leaving trails of red welts. The pressure in her head intensified as his hands tightened around her neck. She felt her lungs screaming for air. Her vision began to blur as she struggled to break free.

Reena threw up her hands, shoving Nasha back as hard as she could before she jumped off the bed, opened the dresser drawer, and poured a salt circle around herself. "Not tonight, motherfucker."

Nasha licked her lips. "Do your worst." She bowed.

"I plan on it." Reena took the doll from the dresser and tossed it next to Nasha. Now that she was in the devil's circle, she couldn't leave it.

Nasha glared at the doll and laughed. "This is all you got?"

Reena pulled the journal page from her back pocket. "Exorcizamus te omnis immundus spiritus," she bellowed.

Nasha scoffed. "That's not gonna work." She reached out and grabbed the doll. "Nasha is my vessel now. I can do whatever the fuck I want." She cackled.

Reena kept speaking the Latin words she believed would work. She had to believe with all her being that these words were not a hoax and that they would bring Nasha back.

Nasha's body twitched. "What are you doing?" She took a step forward but hit an invisible force. Her eyes flared with anger. "I'll fucking kill her!"

Reena didn't stop the Latin words spilling from her mouth as Nasha twitched under them. Nasha raised an arm to her throat.

"I'll kill her. I mean it!" Her head cocked and twitched. "Don't say another word."

Reena spoke louder.

Nasha lowered the knife from her throat. "Reena. I'm here."

Reena fought the urge to look up at her girlfriend, to look into her eyes and hear the softness of her voice, which sounded more Nasha than before.

"Te rogamus, audi nos!" Reena roared.

Nasha's body shook and then collapsed onto the floor. Her eyes rolled to the back of her head.

"I bind you, evil spirit. I bind you to this doll." The doll next to Nasha's body moved slightly. "By air and earth, by water and fire, so be you bound, as I desire. By three and nine, your power I bind. By moon and sun, my will be done." Without hesitation, Reena grabbed the box and wire from the drawer. She wrapped the doll tightly in the iron wire and placed it in the wooden box etched with the sigils painted within the devil's circle. "Sky and sea, keep harm from me. Cord go round. Power be bound, the light revealed, now be sealed." Reena poured salt into the box with one last touch and snapped it shut, ensuring it would never open. She tied the wire around the lock on the outside. With shaky hands, she set the box inside her duffle bag and dropped to her knees beside Nasha's unmoving body.

Tears streaked her face as her hands cupped Nasha's. "You said you were still in there." She sniffled.

Reena stood with determination, carefully cradling Nasha in her arms. The weight of Nasha's body was heavy and unresponsive, and as she took wobbly steps forward, the floor seemed to sway beneath her. She managed two, then three, and finally four shaky strides before gently laying Nasha down onto the full-size bed, its covers inviting yet untouched. She swiftly grabbed the soft throw blanket draped casually over the reading chair beside the dresser, its fabric warm and comforting, and carefully covered Nasha, ensuring she was snug and protected, before sinking onto the edge of the bed.

"Please, be okay," Reena said as she rubbed Nasha's legs.

It's been eleven months. Eleven months of worry. Eleven months of sleepless nights. Eleven months of murder case investigations. Eleven months of following the false news on TV. Eleven months of reading dead-end articles. Eleven months of researching and learning new languages. For eleven months, Reena waited for this moment, but she didn't feel the relief or the joy she had thought she'd feel.

Instead, she was defeated and beaten down. She was a failure for not finding Nasha sooner—eleven months was too much time. Now, her name and face were slandered all over the media. There is no coming back from this.

Epilogue

Together Again

"And that you guys was my experience with the Clown Motel." Reena gave a half smile. "I never found Nasha. So if you are out there somewhere, reach out to me or your family. I miss you." She grabbed a stack of old newspapers and articles and dumped them in the trash. "And that's it for Friends In The Dark, see you next time!" She put her hand over the camera, making it pitch black before cutting it off.

Nasha lowered the camera. "I hate our story."

"It's not the best story, but at least I have you."

Nasha set the camera on the table. "I don't see how you can look at me—how you can still love me."

Reena cupped Nasha's cheek in her hand, turning her head gently to look her in the eyes. "It wasn't you, Nasha."

"I know …" She tried to smile but failed. "I know."

Reena understood that Nasha's ability to embrace life entirely had been irreparably altered; although their ordeal had seemingly concluded, the echoes of trauma lingered. Nasha was plagued by relentless night terrors, her sleep fractured by piercing screams that penetrated the silence of the night. Each time she awoke drenched in cold sweat, her heart racing, it was clear that the struggle was far from over. She often shared her feelings of disconnection, as if her mind and body were foreign entities, still haunted by the remnants of her possession. Reena felt deep sympathy for her friend, recognizing that the journey to reclaim her sense of self would be a long and arduous path filled with shadowy memories that made wholeness seem just out of reach.

"We will go back to our lives when you're ready."

Nasha sighed, sitting on Reena's bed. "I don't want you waiting for me."

"I waited an entire year for you, and I'll wait longer to experience life with you by my side."

Reena meticulously documented her entire harrowing experience on camera. She recorded the chilling possession at the Inn, the terrifying moment when she was attacked, and the intense struggle as she confronted the malevolent entity within Nasha. Each frightening detail was captured. They had decided together they simply couldn't bury the doll and risk someone discovering it and bringing back Amon. So, they kept it locked away while they did research. Finally, they found someone in Nevada who owned a museum of haunted items. He was a collector of all things paranormal and had a team that performed weekly rituals and cleansings to ensure the evil there stayed.

Once Reena and Nasha had decided that was the best option, they drove halfway and met with the team, handing over the box containing the darkest part of their lives. During the short encounter, the team reassured them countless times that the doll would remain locked in the box and safe from the public. Relief washed over Reena more than it did Nasha. Though she agreed to hand it over, half of her wanted to keep the doll within their reach so no one would know the horrors she had lived through.

After the exorcism, a heavy sense of dread hung over Nasha, and she soon fell ill, succumbing to an overwhelming weakness that left her unconscious for days. When she finally regained consciousness, her mind was a chaotic whirlwind of fear and resilience. All of these moments—the terror, the confrontation, and her subsequent recovery—were preserved on a single tape, a hope for justice that Reena clung to as she prepared for what lay ahead. She believed that this tape would serve as undeniable evidence of the horror she had endured.

Nasha was gripped by an overwhelming fear, hesitant to step into the glaring light of truth regarding the entire situation. The thought of being labeled insane and confined to a mental institution haunted her mind. Even worse than the dread that loomed over her was the possibility of her being sentenced to a lifetime in prison.

Reena made the difficult decision to leave Nevada behind after this turmoil. She packed her bags, saying a bittersweet goodbye to her family and friends, convinced that a fresh start was her only option, which wasn't a lie. A lot had happened in Nevada. Her brother was taken from her, she dropped out of college, people gave her weird looks, and she couldn't have Nasha. With the funds she had accrued from her successful YouTube channel, she purchased a charming house tucked away in the serene expanses of rural Tennessee, far removed from the chaos and judgment of her former life.

As she approached the final stages of earning her bachelor's degree, Reena immersed herself in her university coursework, navigating her psychology studies entirely online. She even took Witchcraft in Europe and creative writing classes, as her experience sparked a passion for creatively sharing her story with the world—a way she could tell the whole truth without all the media.

Meanwhile, Nasha embraced her time outdoors, fostering her creativity and practicality. She transformed the backyard into a lively workspace, dedicating herself to reading and constructing various projects to keep her mind engaged and her hands busy. Among her proudest achievements was a charming fire pit surrounded by sturdy wooden benches she crafted herself; each piece told a story of her labor and skill. Nasha had always possessed a natural talent for woodworking, a gift she discovered during her high school wood shop classes, where she honed her abilities and developed a passion for creating with her hands.

The soft glow of the laptop screen bathed Reena's face in a warm light as she clicked 'submit' on her final paper, a weight lifting from her shoulders. 'Just one more semester to go,' she thought, exhilaration bubbling within her. Standing up from her cluttered desk, she went down the dimly lit hallway, the silence wrapping around her like a cozy blanket.

As she reached the end of the corridor, she glanced into the living room and kitchen, both echoing with emptiness. Curiosity tugged at her, prompting her to peer out of the expansive sliding glass door. Nasha was briskly preparing the fire pit with deft hands, her breath visible in the crisp winter air. A smile spread across Reena's face, and she felt a rush of warmth as she turned back to the kitchen.

Grabbing two tall, rustic mugs from the cabinet, Reena swiftly prepared a rich, steaming cup of hot chocolate, the sweet aroma filling the air. With her heart swelling in anticipation, she slid open the glass door, allowing the cool, invigorating winter breeze to caress her skin. Outside, the skeletal trees swayed gently, their branches rustling softly in the light wind, while the heavy clouds drifted lazily across the night sky, obscuring the glimmering stars above.

Settling onto the sturdy wooden bench beside Nasha, Reena handed her a mug. They sat together in companionable silence, the crackling of the flames punctuating the peaceful evening. Both savored the moment and the promise of the adventures yet to come.

Nasha put her head on Reena's shoulder and sighed. "Thank you for fighting for me."

"I promised I'd find you." Reena rested her head on Nasha's. "Happy Valentine's Day, my love."

Also By

Maple Ridge Duet:
The Scholars Gambit
Book 2 -TBA

Anthology:
Hallow 13

Short Stories:
The Lurkers: A Short Story of Maggie & Harold

About the Author

 Twyla is a mother to three wild boys and two lovable fur babies. As a full-time college student, she balances life with a dose of caffeine and chaos. When not writing or studying, she finds joy in the great outdoors and reading.

Social media:
Instagram: @twyla.mp.writes
Tiktok: @parker.writes
Facebook: Author Twyla Menezes
Website: https://author-twyla-menezes.company.site/

Made in the USA
Monee, IL
18 May 2025